Wish
Come
True
Cat

To Thomas James, with love
~ RS
For Mum and Dad
~ GH

ISBN 0-439-46611-3

Text copyright © 2001 by Ragnhild Scamell.
Illustrations copyright © 2001 by Gaby Hansen.
All rights reserved.
Published by Scholastic Inc., 557 Broadway, New York, NY 10012,
by arrangement with Barron's Educational Series, Inc.
SCHOLASTIC and associated logos are trademarks and/or registered trademarks of Scholastic Inc.

12 11 10 9 8 7 6 5 4 3 2 1   2 3 4 5 6 7/0

Printed in the U.S.A.   14

First Scholastic printing, September 2002

Wish Come True Cat

Ragnhild Scamell

illustrated by Gaby Hansen

SCHOLASTIC INC.

New York Toronto London Auckland Sydney
Mexico City New Delhi Hong Kong Buenos Aires

Holly's house had a cat door.
It was a small door in the
big door so a cat could come
and go.

But Holly didn't have a cat.

One night, something magical
happened. Holly saw a falling star.

As the star trailed across the sky, she
made a wish.
"I wish I had a kitten," she whispered.
"A tiny cuddly kitten who could jump
in and out of the cat door."

CRASH!

Something big landed on the windowsill outside.

It wasn't a kitten . . .

It was Tom, the scruffiest, most raggedy cat Holly had ever seen. He sat there in the moonlight, smiling a crooked smile.

"Meo-o-ow!"

"I'm Tom, your wish come true cat," he seemed to say.

"It's a mistake," cried Holly.
"I wished for a kitten."
Tom didn't think Holly had
made a mistake.

He rubbed his torn ear
against the window and
howled so loudly it made
him cough and splutter.

"Meo-o-ow, o-o-w, o-o-w!"

Holly hid under her
quilt, hoping that
he'd go away.

The next morning, Tom was still there, waiting for her outside the cat door. He wanted to come in, and he had brought her a present of a smelly old piece of fish.

"Yuk!" said Holly. She picked
it up and dropped it in the
garbage can. Tom looked
puzzled.
"Bad cat," she said, shooing
him away.

"Go on, go home!" said
Holly, walking across
to her swing.

But Tom was there before
her. He sharpened his
claws on the swing . . .

and washed his coat
noisily, pulling out bits
of fur and spitting them
everywhere.

At lunchtime, Tom sat on the
windowsill, watching Holly eat.

She broke off a piece of her sandwich and passed it out to him through the cat door. Tom wolfed it down, purring all the while.

In the afternoon, a cold wind swept through
the garden, and Holly had to wear her jacket
and scarf. Tom didn't seem to feel the cold.
He followed her around . . .

chasing leaves . . .

balancing along the
top of the fence . . .

showing off.

Soon it was time for Holly to go
indoors for dinner.
"'Bye then, Tom," she said, and
stroked his scruffy head.

Tom followed her across to the **door**
and settled himself by the cat door.

That evening, it snowed.
Gleaming pompoms of
snow danced in the air.
Outside the cat door,
Tom curled himself into a
ragged ball to keep warm.
Soon there was a white
cushion of snow all over
the doorstep, and on Tom.

Holly heard him meowing
miserably. She ran to the
cat door and held it open . . .

Tom came in, shaking snow all over the kitchen floor.

"Poor old Tom," said Holly.

He ate a large plate of food, and drank an even larger bowl of warm milk.

Tom purred louder than ever when Holly dried him with the kitchen towel.

Soon Tom had settled down,
snug on Holly's bed.
Holly stroked his scruffy fur,
and together they watched
the glittering stars.

Then, suddenly, another star
fell. Holly couldn't think of
a single thing to wish for.
She had everything she
wanted. And so had Tom.